Fox

and the spots

Colin and Jacqui Hawkins

Collins

An Imprint of HarperCollins*Publishers*

Foxy was bored.
He had nothing to do.

2.

He didn't want to play with his toys.

He didn't want to watch television.
"I'm fed up," said Foxy.
And he wouldn't eat his supper.

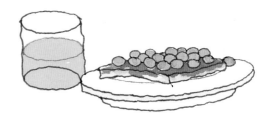

Foxy felt hot, sick and grumpy.
"I've got a headache,"
he groaned.
He didn't want to do
anything.

Foxy didn't want to go to bed, but he soon fell asleep.

The next morning Foxy was
covered in spots.
"I'm so itchy," he cried.
Poor Foxy had chickenpox.

Foxy stayed in bed all day.
His little sister looked
after him.
"I'll make you better,"
she said.

Soon Foxy did
feel a lot
better.

But now his little sister
was feeling grumpy.

Brrring! The doorbell rang.

It was Badger and Dog.
"Hello, Foxy," said
Badger.

"Are you spotty, too?"
said Dog.

"We're all spotty," giggled Foxy.

The spotty friends played
football until tea time.

They all felt a lot better.

At tea time everyone ate
spotty cake.

"Look who's spotty now,"
said Foxy.

And they all laughed.

Read more about Foxy and friends in
FOXY LOSES HIS TAIL

First published in Great Britain by HarperCollins Publishers Ltd in 1995 ISBN 0 00 198146 3 (hardback) 10 9 8 7 6 5 4 3 2 1
ISBN 0 00 664537 2 (paperback) 10 9 8 7 6 5 4 3 2 1 Text and illustrations copyright © Colin and Jacqui Hawkins 1995
The authors assert the moral right to be identified as the authors of this work. A CIP catalogue record for this title is available
from the British Library. All rights reserved. No part of the publication may be reproduced, stored in a retrieval system,
or transmitted in any form or by any means, electronic, mechanical, photocopying, recording or otherwise, without the
prior permission of HarperCollins Publishers Ltd, 77-85 Fulham Palace Road, Hammersmith, London W6 8JB
Printed and bound in